teddy bears
take the train

susanna gretz · alison sage

Four Winds Press New York

Charles has planned our route already,
Robert holds his compass steady,
And Louise has her umbrella for the rain!

*To be sung to the tune of *She'll Be Comin' Round The Mountain*.

Four Winds Press
Macmillan Publishing Company
866 Third Avenue, New York, NY 10022
Collier Macmillan Canada, Inc.

Printed in Hong Kong by Dai Nippon Printing Co. Ltd.
First published 1987 by A & C Black (Publishers) Ltd.,
London
First Four Winds Press edition 1987

10 9 8 7 6 5 4 3 2 1

Library of Congress Cataloging-in-Publication Data
Gretz, Susanna. Teddy bears take the train.
Summary: The teddy bears' train trip to see Uncle
Jerome is filled with songs, games, and surprises.
[1. Railroads–Trains–Fiction.   2. Teddy bears–
Fiction]   I. Sage, Alison.   II. Title.
PZ7.G8636Tfg   1987   [E]   87–8572
ISBN 0-02-738170-6

Sara was reading a letter.
Louise, Robert, and Charles were listening.
So was Fred, the dog.

we'll meet you at
BEARHAMPTON STATION
at 2 O'CLOCK. Great-Uncle
can't wait to see you all.
love,
ANDREW
John   William
and Great-Uncle Jerome

"We'd better start packing," said Charles.

"I don't like your Great-Uncle Jerome," said Louise.
"Why not?" said Robert. "He's got a pond at the
   bottom of his garden and a telescope. I like him."
"But he never hears anything you say," said Louise,
   "and there are frogs in the bath . . .

sleeping bag
rock collection
bug jar
bug box
magnifying glass
toothbrush
spider book

"AND it always rains when we go to see him."
"I was going to take my swimming things," said Sara.
"Don't bother," said Louise.
"Stop it, Louise!" said Charles.
"Just think, we're going by TRAIN!"

The four bears packed their things.
"Hurry," said Sara.
"We're going to be late."

At the station, the line for
tickets was very long.
"Hurry!" said Sara.
"We're going to miss that train."

Waiting at the platform were two trains.
"Not that red train, Louise," said Charles.
"This blue one's ours."
"Yuk. The red one's much better,"
  grumbled Louise.
"I like the blue one," said Charles.

"Stop fussing!" said Sara. "*Do* hurry up!"
The guard was blowing his whistle.
"I *hate* hurrying," said Louise.

Everyone scrambled into the train.
It moved slowly out of the station.
"It's full," grumbled Louise.
"No," said Charles,
"there's just enough room for all of us."
"But look who's sitting over there,"
said Louise. "White bears!"

"Well?" said Charles.
"I don't like white bears,"
 said Louise.
"Shhh!" said Charles.
"Don't stare."
"Let's play a train game,"
 suggested Sara.

I packed my bag and in it I put . . .

"But, really, I forgot my fishing rod," said Robert.
"Never mind," said Charles. "Let's go on with the game."

"I forgot that, too," moaned Robert.
"Never mind," said the ticket collector, as he punched all their tickets.

Meanwhile, the white bears
were opening several large
box lunches.
"What are they eating?"
whispered Robert.
"Probably fried worms,"
said Louise. "Or spiders."
The little white bears took
out bottles of juice and
stared at Louise.
"Shhh!" said Sara.
"Let's have *our* picnic,"
said Charles.

HOT SANDWICHES
Egg on Toast
Grilled Cheese

COLD SANDWICHES
Cheese + Tomato
Egg salad
Peanut butter + jam

COLD DRINKS
Orange juice
Lemonade · Cola
Raspberry Fizz
Black currant juice

HOT
Choc
Tea
Milk

While Charles unpacked the food,
Robert and Sara went to the buffet
for drinks and paper napkins.

When they had finished eating, Louise went off
to explore the train.
"Don't be long," said Sara. "We have to get off soon."

Louise looked at the other passengers.

She looked out at the woods and fields and houses.

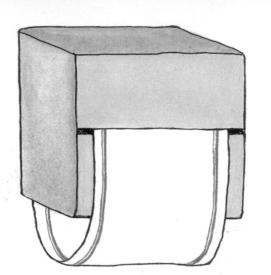

Then she found the bathroom.
She went in, and the door
swung shut.
She pulled it,
but it wouldn't move.
She was locked in.

"I wonder where Louise is?" said Robert.
They hunted up and down the train.
Fred hunted, too.
"Where *is* she?" said Sara.

Where *was* she?

Just then they heard a loud banging noise.
"Let me out," shouted a voice.
"I'm IN HERE!"

First they pulled
the door handle.
That didn't work.

Then Charles wiggled the door
sideways on its hinges.
That didn't work, either.

Then they poked a
train ticket and a spoon
in the lock.
The lock chewed up the ticket
and twisted the spoon.
But the door stayed shut.

Suddenly, there was a loud
crackling noise:

ZZZ OOH PASSENGERS WHOO LUGGAGE ZZ
AS WE SHALL SHORTLY BE ARRIVING AT CRKK ZZZZZ

"Help!" yelled Louise.
"I'll be stuck in here
forever!"

"Excuse me," said a quiet voice.
"Can I help?"
It was one of the white bears.
"Listen," said the white bear
to Louise.
"Take some soap from the basin
and rub it on the bolt.
It must be jammed.
Now, while you pull the bolt
we'll try to lift the door a little."

"Everyone, all together, LIFT!"

There was a scrunching sound as the bolt slid back . . .

and the door swung open.
"Hooray!" shouted everyone
except Louise.
"Thank you," she mumbled.
"Not at all,"
said the white bear.

The train stopped with a jerk.
"We're here!" shouted Robert.
"We'll never make it," cried Sara.
They bundled all their bags
out to the platform, helped by
the friendly white bears.

Bearhamptor

"Keep the rest of our sandwiches,"
said Sara.
"That's very kind but no, thank you,"
said the white bears.
"We don't eat seaweed."

Bearhampton

The train was pulling out of the station.
"Seaweed?" shouted Robert.
"That's not seaweed – it's lettuce!"
But the smiling white bears didn't hear him.

Louise gave Great-Uncle Jerome a hug.
"You won't believe how glad I am to be here," she said.
"Bees? Did you say *bees here?*" said Great-Uncle Jerome.
"I don't have any bees, only a frog."
"It's true," said John.
"Great-Uncle *has* got a frog in the bath.
   He really has."

Sara's Song*

Oh, we're off to see Great-Uncle on the train,

We're not traveling by bus or boat or plane,